Return of the Undead

Can you destroy the Vampire of Valdah?

Allen Sharp

Cambridge University Press

Cambridge
London   New York   New Rochelle
Melbourne   Sydney

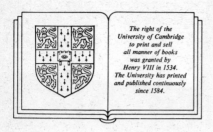

The right of the University of Cambridge to print and sell all manner of books was granted by Henry VIII in 1534. The University has printed and published continuously since 1584.

Published by the Press Syndicate of the University of Cambridge
The Pitt Building, Trumpington Street, Cambridge CB2 1RP
32 East 57th Street, New York, NY 10022, USA
296 Beaconsfield Parade, Middle Park, Melbourne 3206, Australia

© Cambridge University Press 1984

First published 1984

Printed in Great Britain by the Guernsey Press Co. Ltd, Guernsey,
Channel Islands

Library of Congress catalogue card number: 83–25193

British Library cataloguing in publication data
Sharp, Allen
Return of the Undead – (Storytrails)
I. Title II. Series
823′.914 J PZ7
ISBN 0 521 27709 4

Storytrails by Allen Sharp

DS

Cover and inside illustration by John Storey
Embellishments by Celia Hart

Read this first

This book may be like no book that you have read before, because **you** decide the story. It is just like having an adventure in real life. What happens in the book happens to **you**. You decide what to do next and, like a real-life adventure, the end may not always be a happy one. That is up to **you**.

There are plenty of thrills and scares and you will have lots of chances to decide what you would do if you were really caught up in the adventure.

You are on a walking holiday with two friends in Romania. One evening, as you make for the town of Sabrov, you find that you have lost your way. A storm drives you to take shelter in a strange house. As your adventure unfolds you find that you are in a place where the people still believe the legend of the vampires; the 'undead' who stalk the night to feed on the blood of unwary humans. But is it only a legend? What terrors would you face to save a friend from death at the hands of a demon that thirsts only for blood? To find out, you have only to follow the simple instructions printed opposite.

How to use your book

The left-hand pages of this book are numbered in the top left-hand corner. Flick the edge of your book through your fingers and you will see that the numbers are easy to find.

You start reading on the page marked 1 and when you come to the end of the opposite page it will tell you where to go next. As you go through the book, there will be times when you have to make a choice about what to do next. As you come to the end of the page you will see what the choice is. You choose what you are going to do by turning to the number of the page shown in brackets beside your choice.

Example: '"Turn back now," the priest said, "and I think we will be safe." **(21)** "Go on, and I will pray for us." **(26)**'

If you decide to turn back, then you will turn to page 21. If you decide to go on, then you will turn to page 26.

To be completely successful on your adventure, you must destroy the 'Vampire of Valdah', but without being destroyed yourself! If you fail the first time, you can always try again.

Now turn to page 1.

1

The sun had still not set but the sky had been dark for the last two hours. The air was warm and clammy. Far to the south, beyond the peaks of the Carpathian Mountains, there was an almost continuous flicker of sheet lightning.

Our last few days had been dogged by heavy thunderstorms and it looked as if yet another was on its way. We had been due to reach the town of Sabrov early that evening, but there was only empty road and dark forest ahead of us.

Eric stopped and took out the map. He spread it out on the grass verge and Martha and I knelt on either side of him. There was just enough light to read it.

'There's Sabrov,' Eric said, 'and there's the road that we should be on.'

'More to the point,' said Martha, impatiently, 'which road are we on and exactly where are we?'

Eric wasn't sure. It was a situation I should have been getting used to. I had spent the last two summers walking with Eric and his sister, Martha Hoffman. Eric had already proved his ability to get us lost just about anywhere in Europe, from the Black Forest to the middle of Paris! This time, it was somewhere in Romania!

I looked at the map myself. I thought I could see where we had made the wrong turning. If I was right, we were walking away from Sabrov and the nearest bit of civilisation was a small village called Valdah. It was five kilometres off and on the other side of the forest.

Now it had started to rain. As Eric hurried to fold up the map, a brilliant fork of lightning lit up the whole landscape. I saw that Martha was pointing, though her words were drowned by a roll of thunder almost overhead. She tried again.

'There's a house,' she shouted. 'At least, it's a building of some sort. I saw the windows in that lightning flash. I can't see it now, but it's just up the hillside through the trees.'

We struck off in the direction Martha had pointed. A hundred metres brought us onto a rough driveway. It looked as though it had not been used for a long time. The house would probably be the same!

Turn to page 2.

2

The house was not the same. It was worse! It might once have been big enough to be called a 'castle', but almost half of it had been burned down and the part that remained was in a sorry state. Still, it could mean shelter of sorts.

We crossed a weed-filled courtyard. The centre of the house and one wing were still standing. Eric suggested that we split up and try to find an open window. Martha was a little way ahead.

'No need,' she called back to us, 'the door is open.'

Once through the door, we were looking into almost total darkness. Eric struck a match which instantly blew out in the draught. He was trying again when the whole scene was suddenly lit by a whole series of flashes. It was still too quick to take everything in, but one thing was certain. The house may have been derelict, but it was still furnished! I had caught a glimpse of a candlestick, filled with half-burned candles on a table by the door. I waited for the next flash and grabbed it. I shouted to Martha to close the door and to Eric to strike another match. The candles were lit and I held them high so that we might inspect the room.

Cobwebs hung from the lofty ceiling and from the walls but, when I looked down at my feet, I saw that the floor was free of dust. It had been swept! Eric had moved further into the room.

'The big table in the centre,' he said, 'has been dusted – and the logs in the hearth look freshly laid.'

'I don't like it,' Martha said. 'Someone must be living here. I think we should go.'

'Nonsense!' replied Eric. 'If someone is living here, then so much the better. All we've got is some chocolate and biscuits. I wouldn't mind a proper meal.'

He found more candles, and now with his own light walked to the foot of what had been a grand staircase leading to the upper parts of the house.

'Hallo!' he shouted. 'Is anyone at home?'

Only his own voice came echoing back and a muffled scrabbling from behind the wood panelling. It looked like our only company was rats (3)!

3

'That's it!' Martha exclaimed. 'I don't like the feel of the place. I don't like the idea of staying here uninvited. And I'm not staying in a place with rats! I'd rather get wet!'

With that, she opened the door behind her.

The flashes of lightning now lit a flooded court-yard. Rain lashed through the open doorway and a violent gust of wind almost swept her off her feet. I helped her to shut the door again. All the candles had blown out except the one that Eric was still holding.

Martha's voice, less confident now, came from the darkness.

'On second thoughts, I'm staying!'

Eric relit the candles and started a fire in the huge hearth. The flames made the place look almost cheerful.

We ate what food we had and sat in front of the fire. Eric had been staring around the huge room.

'What do you know about art?' he asked me.

'A little,' I answered. 'I've seen most of the

great galleries of Europe and you know that I have an uncle who deals in works of fine art. Why?'

'Take a walk across the room and look at those pictures on the wall opposite.'

I did as Eric asked. There was a Turner and a Goya. They certainly looked like originals and, if they were, must have been worth a fortune.

'They are originals?' Eric asked.

'Yes,' I replied. 'I think so – or very good fakes.'

'Look at the candlestick you're holding. It's solid silver and looks very old. I think the place must be a treasure house, yet there's no-one here and the door was open.'

Eric was right. The more one saw of the house the stranger it seemed.

'I suggest we explore,' Eric said.

'I'm not leaving this room,' Martha insisted.

'All right,' Eric answered and looked at me. 'You toss a coin. If it's heads, you take downstairs (5). If it's tails you take upstairs (7). Agreed?'

I agreed and took out a coin.

4

I was almost surprised to find Martha sleeping quietly by the fire. Eric was coming down the stairs and joined me.

'Martha's asleep,' I said. 'I would have thought she'd be too nervous to sleep.'

Eric shrugged his shoulders.

'That heavy cold she had when we started the holiday – I don't think she's really got over it. She puts on a brave face, but I've seen her looking tired a few times.'

Martha stirred, opened her eyes, and looked at us.

'I'm sorry,' she said. 'I must have dozed off.'

'There's a bed upstairs,' Eric told her. 'It's spotlessly clean – and when you see the bedroom, I don't think you'd want to miss the chance of sleeping in it. It has a very thick oak door and if you're nervous, you can lock yourself in.'

I expected Martha to argue. She didn't. All she said was, 'What about you two?'

Before I could answer, Eric had assured her that we had somewhere to sleep. He turned to me.

'I'll take her up,' he said, 'and join you back here in a moment.'

I was left alone by the fire while Eric took Martha upstairs. Shortly, he returned.

'I'm sorry,' he said, 'if you felt that I was taking things over, but I'm sure there's someone else in the house.'

I said that I agreed with him.

'Martha can get nervous of her own shadow. Locked away upstairs is the safest place for her to be. I know that you don't frighten too easily.'

I was grateful for Eric's compliment. I wasn't sure that he was right! I asked him what he had in mind.

'If we arrange some chairs by the fire, one of us can try to get some sleep while the other keeps watch. It's nearly midnight. Say eight hours – two hours on watch, two off – 'till morning.'

It sounded a sensible suggestion.

'I seem to have been making all the decisions. You choose who takes first watch, you (8), or me (6).'

5

Eric took some candles and made his way up the staircase. There were several doors leading off the room we were in. The first two that I tried seemed to have been nailed up and I guessed that they led to the part of the house that had been destroyed by fire.

The next opened into a library. Its shelves were still filled with books though, unlike the room I had come from, the whole place was covered in dust and cobwebs. I pulled some of the cobwebs away to read the book titles. It was obviously a fine, if curious collection; some rare early works on magic, many hand written on vellum, works on science and philosophy, some very old. Though I could only glance briefly at a tiny sample, the library also seemed to house all the great works of literature from Homer to Dickens.

I was still pondering on who could have owned such a collection when I found my way to the kitchens. Brown, furry bodies scattered into the darkness as the light of my candles spread over the stone floor.

There was a sudden crash of breaking crockery.

I stood still, straining my ears against the constant rumble of the storm outside. There was a light click and then the creak of boards. Then there was nothing. I raised the candles.

In front of me was a table with the remains of a meal on it – cheese and black bread. The bread felt moist and the cheese still soft. Something crunched under my foot. I looked down. A pool of milk was spreading out from the broken pieces of an earthenware pitcher. The place smelt of rotting food. I need explore no more to tell Eric that we would not be eating breakfast in the kitchens! There was no doubt that someone used the house, though surely not the person who had collected the art treasures or the fine library.

I was turning back when the light of the candles fell on another door. I opened it to find a narrow, wooden staircase beyond. I remembered the click, perhaps of a latch, and the creak of boards. Was someone else in the house? I would sleep happier if I knew. Should I go up the stairs (9), or return to Martha, who was alone and probably getting nervous (4)?

6

I settled down to sleep leaving Eric sitting by the fire.

I woke with a start as a log settled on the fire and burst into a crackle of sparks and flame. Eric was slouched in a chair opposite to me, and sound asleep. The storm was over, but the silence which now filled the house was almost more unnerving. A big, pale yellow moon with thin clouds scudding across its face, shone through the high, arched window above the staircase. It filled the room with moving shadows adding to my sense of unease in the unnatural silence. I looked at the time. It was four thirty in the morning.

Eric must have gone to sleep during his watch. I had missed my watch completely. Really it was Eric's turn again, but I decided that I would do the next two hours.

I was still feeling sleepy and the warmth of the fire was not helping me stay awake. I got up and walked upstairs so that I could look out of the window.

The moon lit a view across a broken terrace, what must have been lawns and flower beds beyond, and on to the very edge of the forest. A thin mist just covered the ground, strangely still below the fast moving clouds.

As I watched I thought I saw a figure moving away from the house towards the forest. It was difficult to follow the movement in the light and shade of the moonlight. Now, it looked like two figures, one some way ahead of the other; the farthest like the figure of a girl, the other either someone very small or following in a crouched position for fear of being seen. Then they vanished as a larger cloud covered the moon.

I couldn't swear to what I had seen but I took my candles up to Martha's room and tried the door. It was still locked.

By six o'clock the sun was well up and I was beginning to nod off. Eric was still sleeping as soundly as ever.

I wondered whether to wake him so that he could see out the rest of the time until Martha appeared (15). It looked a bright morning. A walk around outside might do me more good than going to sleep again (13).

7

I didn't like the idea of going upstairs alone, but 'tails' it had been. I took up my candles and mounted the wide staircase.

At the head of the stairs was a corridor which led off in two directions. From where I stood, I could see that one direction was blocked off by a rough wall of brick and plaster. I guessed that it must once have led to the part of the house which had burned down. I took the opposite direction, stopping at each of the several rooms in turn.

Some were empty. Some were furnished. All were thick with years of dust. I found a bathroom, of sorts. With everything, including the walls and floor, made of green marble, it must once have been palatial – and someone had begun to clean it. The work had not got far, but around the clean patches were what looked like hand prints. They were tiny, like a child's and there was something else odd about them. They were all of a right hand!

I left the bathroom and reached the last door before the corridor made a sharp turn to the right. I pushed it open and stood there, just gazing in astonishment. The room was spotless. It was dominated by a huge four-poster bed, covered in crisp, fresh linen and hung with fine brocade curtains. The bed and all the rest of the furniture in the room looked as though they were from an old French castle.

I walked into the room to take a closer look around. Through a window across the corridor, a bright flash of lightning threw the shape of the doorway onto the wall opposite – the doorway, and the shape of someone standing in it!

I whipped around. The doorway was empty. When I reached it, so was the corridor. Was there someone else in the house? If there was, he or she had vanished so quickly that they must have disappeared round the bend in the corridor. I hesitated to follow. Should I call Eric so we could search together (10)? I suddenly thought of Martha who could be alone downstairs! Ought I to go back to her (12)?

8

I had chosen first watch because, though I was tired, I didn't see myself sleeping through the noise of the storm. Eric seemed quite happy to try, stretched himself out across three chairs and, very soon, looked as if he had fallen asleep.

I sat for a while by the fire, only to find myself nodding off. I got up and walked part of the way upstairs. From the half landing, with its large arched window, I could see a broken terrace leading down to what must once have been grand lawns and flower beds. At times, the landscape was lit so brightly, I could see as far as the edge of the forest. I had never seen a storm of quite such fury. The sky was almost continuously broken by jagged flashes of light. Sparks of every colour splattered across the ground and cascaded down in great showers from treetops and stonework alike. Somewhere on the edge of the forest, a ball of white light turned to orange, then red as a tree blazed up, only to be quenched by the deluge of rain.

It was as the glow of red was fading that I heard what I thought was someone calling Martha's name. I looked down the stairs at Eric. The flames of the fire still burned brightly and Eric was surely asleep.

'Martha!'

The voice was clear in my head, yet seemed to come from some great distance. I took the candles and ran to Martha's room. The door was locked. I tapped on it lightly, but there was no sound from within. I went back to the stairs and waited. The call was not repeated. I told myself it was only the effect of the wind and my overworked imagination. I returned to the fire where Eric still slept and, for a long time, sat listening.

I must have fallen asleep for, when I woke, the sun was streaming in through the open door. Eric had gone. I called out, but he didn't reply. I looked at my watch. It was almost seven in the morning!

Should I check that Martha was still safely locked in her room (11), or look for Eric who, from the open door, might well have taken a walk outside (13)?

9

As I mounted the stairs, I became aware of a light somewhere above me. I called out, 'Is that you Eric?' There was no answer and the light instantly vanished.

At the top of the stairs I found a second door, leading to a corridor. There was a faint smell of wax, as if candles had just been snuffed out. I called Eric's name again. This time, there was a reply from somewhere down the corridor.

'I'm still in the bedroom. I told you I'd wait for you while you brought Martha.'

I hurried towards the voice. I turned a corner to see light coming from an open door. The house seemed never-ending in its surprises. Eric was standing in the centre of one of the most elegant bedrooms I had ever seen. It was dominated by a great four-poster bed, its draperies spotless, its bed linen crisp and clean. All the furnishing was very old and ornate, and the carpet was thick and richly coloured.

'Where did you get to?' Eric asked, 'and where's Martha?'

'I'm sorry,' I said, 'but I don't know what you're talking about. I've just come up the back stairs from the kitchen.'

Eric looked at me, obviously disbelieving.

'Stop it!' he said. 'It's my sister that's the nervous one. It won't work with me. I saw you come to the door and I asked you to fetch Martha. Since you went straight off, I assumed that was what you were doing.'

'You "saw" me come to the door?' I repeated.

'Well . . . yes. I mean I was too interested in this room to be staring at you, but I heard you and caught a glimpse of you in the doorway. It had to be you. There are only the three of us in the house.'

Eric was watching my face.

'You weren't joking, were you?' he said after a pause. 'It wasn't you at the door?'

I shook my head.

'All right,' he said. 'We say nothing to Martha. You go downstairs. I'll get the candles from the table over there and follow you down.'(4)

10

I called Eric's name as loudly as I could, not knowing where he might be in the house, but hoping he would hear. Seconds went by and I heard steps behind me. I turned to see Martha.

'What's wrong?' she asked. 'I heard you calling for Eric. I don't know where he is, but you sounded as if you might be in trouble.'

There was no time to answer her before there were more footsteps; this time from around the corner of the corridor. Instinctively, I stepped back, colliding with Martha.

'What's the matter with you?' she asked. 'You're trembling. It's only Eric. Who were you expecting?'

It was Eric.

'I was in the kitchens,' he said. 'I heard you shouting. There's a back stair leading onto the end of this corridor. So what is it?'

It was obvious that neither of them could have passed anyone on the way. I began to doubt my own senses.

'Nothing!' I lied. 'I just wanted Eric to see this room. I didn't think that you, Martha, would want to come upstairs by yourself.'

I don't know whether Martha heard me. She had already stepped into the grand bedroom.

'I've always wanted to sleep in a room like this!' she exclaimed. 'Do you think I could?'

'Why not?' I answered, quickly. 'Lock yourself in and you've got the safest and best place in the house for the night. I know Eric would rather sleep by the fire – and I don't like four-posters. They make me feel hemmed in.'

Eric gave me an odd look, but he knew it was settled. When we were alone again, downstairs by the fire, I made my explanations.

'I'm sorry,' I told him. 'I could think of no other way of getting Martha safely out of harm's way. I don't think we're alone in the house. I don't pretend to be brave, but I don't get hysterical like Martha! I think that we two must keep watch tonight.'

'I agree,' Eric replied. 'I haven't seen anything, but several times I've had the feeling we're not alone. Do you want to take first watch (**8**), or second (**6**)?'

11

Martha's door was still locked. I saw no reason to wake her and returned downstairs, intending to find Eric.

I did not have far to look. Eric was standing in the open doorway. I was feeling a little ashamed of falling asleep on my watch and told him so.

'There is no need for apology,' he said. 'I slept right through the night. I woke only a little while ago, checked that Martha was still in her room and went outside to take a look around in the daylight.'

As he moved into the room from the doorway, I saw that he was limping. He saw me looking.

'It's nothing,' he said. 'I've twisted my ankle on one of the broken stones on the courtyard. The pain will go off.'

Ten minutes later, it had not 'gone off' and Eric was sitting down massaging his ankle when Martha appeared. I thought she looked, somehow, different. For a start, she was wearing a dress, which she never did for walking. It was always jeans. Her dark hair looked untidy and her face was unusually pale.

'You're wearing a dress,' Eric said.

'Because my jeans are wet!' Martha snapped back.

'But they were dry when you went to bed,' Eric retorted.

'They are wet now. When I got up, they were wet, together with all the other clothes I had on last night. And don't ask me how. I don't know. I'm not feeling too good in health or temper. This place may be full of treasures, but there's not a single mirror in the house.'

I could see the beginning of a brother and sister quarrel. I changed the subject by asking Eric what he'd found on his walk outside.

'Nothing much,' was the reply. 'There's a coach house with a coach and carriage in it – and an old hand cart which must have been here when the house was burned – it's very charred.'

I could see that he was more interested in his ankle which had begun to swell. He wasn't going to be able to walk far on it. It looked as if I was going to have to walk to Valdah for help (**14**) leaving Eric and Martha behind. But we might all be able to leave together if we used the old hand cart Eric had seen in the coach house (**16**).

12

I need not have worried. Martha appeared to have dozed off by the fire. I was wondering whether to wake her when I saw Eric coming down the stairs.

'I thought that you were somewhere downstairs,' I said.

'I was,' he replied, 'in the kitchens – and I don't think I was alone! There's a back staircase from the kitchens to the first floor. I think I surprised someone in the middle of a meal and he or she took off up the back stairs. I followed, but I lost whoever it was.'

I told him that I was sure he was right about there being someone else in the house. I asked him if he'd seen the magnificent bedroom.

'Yes,' he answered, 'and I know what you're thinking. If we can persuade Martha to sleep there, it's one way of keeping her safely out of the way.'

It wasn't what I'd been thinking, but it sounded like a sensible idea.

'Sleep where?' said Martha, half waking from her nap by the fire.

Eric told her about the bedroom. I expected her not to want to leave the fire, but I could see that Martha's curiosity was stronger than her fears. She couldn't wait for Eric to show her what we'd found.

Eric returned alone having succeeded in his plan.

'She's locked herself in,' he told me, 'so we can assume that we don't have Martha to worry about for the rest of the night. She did ask where we would sleep. I told her that I preferred the fire and that you couldn't sleep in four-poster beds. They made you feel hemmed in.'

Eric seemed to have thought of everything. I wondered what was coming next.

'I suggest that we take it in turns to keep watch. It's nearly midnight. We've got eight hours – say two on and two off. I'll pull some chairs together by the fire so that whoever's not on watch can get some sort of sleep. I don't mind who does first watch. So you choose. Do you want to do the first two hours (8), or would you rather I did (6)?'

13

Except for a pool of water on the broken courtyard, there were few signs of the storm of the night. I walked to the end of the building where a wide archway led into a yard with a coach house and stables. The stables were empty. The coach house was not.

It contained a coach and a carriage, neglected, but in good condition. The doors of the coach carried a crest visible only in outline beneath the dirt. As I stepped forward to take a closer look I almost fell over an old hand cart. The wood was badly charred as if it had been in a fire but, unlike the coach and carriage, it had been used recently. Not only was it clean, but the metal hoops on the wheels were bright and free of rust. I would have spent more time in the coach house, but I heard Eric shouting my name.

I found him standing in the doorway to the house.

'I've done a stupid thing!' he said.

'If you mean about being asleep when we should have been on watch, perhaps neither of us did too well!' I replied.

'Not that,' Eric said. 'It's my ankle. I slipped on one of those broken stones and I've twisted it. I can hardly bear my weight on it.'

As I helped Eric indoors and to a chair, Martha appeared. We must both have stared at her. She was pale and unusually untidy.

'I know I'm wearing my best dress,' she said. 'My jeans and the rest of the clothes I had on last night are soaking wet. That bedroom must leak . . . and I can't find a mirror in this house. What's the matter with your foot, Eric?'

Eric's ankle was beginning to swell. He wasn't going to be able to walk far on it. Martha didn't look very well either. Even if nothing terrible had happened to us through the night, there was still something very strange about this house. I didn't really want to leave Eric and Martha alone there, but it might be best if I walked to Valdah to get some help (**14**). On the other hand, there might be a way of our leaving together. I was thinking about the cart in the coach house (**16**).

14

With Martha's help, I could certainly have pushed Eric to Valdah on the cart, but the more I looked at Martha, the more I wondered whether she could make the journey herself, let alone help push a heavy cart.

There was nothing left to eat, so I set off at once. I found the driveway by which we had reached the house the night before. I saw that there was also a narrower path which could be a short cut to the road.

I had walked some way along the path before I smelled burning and saw smoke drifting across the path ahead of me. I knew that I should waste no time, but it seemed odd that anything should be burning after so much rain – unless someone was camping among the trees.

In no more than a few steps, I came into a small clearing. At the end of it was a wide stream. Beyond the stream was a graveyard. It was completely overgrown with thorn and ivy, and looked as though it had been undisturbed, perhaps for centuries. The smoke came from the remains of an ancient oak tree in the graveyard, a victim of the night's storm. Its branches lay broken around it.

The gnarled trunk was split apart and still smouldering at its centre. Beside it was a heap of fresh earth, as if the bolt of lightning which had struck the tree had also scooped a great hole in the ground.

Curiosity prompted me to move nearer. Standing by the edge of the stream, I could see that the water forked both upstream and downstream from where I stood. The graveyard was an island. Then how was it reached? There must, at one time, have been a bridge to it. I walked far enough in both directions to see right round it. There was no bridge and no sign of there ever having been one.

With another mystery to add to those of the night, I knew that I should be making haste to Valdah. As I was turning away, I saw something in the mud of the bank opposite: two sets of footprints. One was of a tiny foot. The other was of a walking shoe with a very distinctive pattern on its sole. Martha had just such a pair of shoes!

I had not liked leaving Eric and Martha alone. Now I was sure I must return to the house (**20**).

15

Eric grunted a few times as I shook him and, eventually opened his eyes. Realising that it was morning, he sat bolt upright, a worried expression on his face.

'It's morning!' he said. 'What happened?'

'Nothing,' I replied, 'except that you must have gone to sleep on your watch and failed to wake me. I did wake at about four thirty and have sat here for most of the time since.'

'I'm sorry,' Eric said, rubbing the sleep from his eyes. 'I suppose Martha's all right?'

I told him that I had checked her room through the night and that the door was still locked. I had been awake since then and I had neither seen nor heard anything unusual.

Stretching himself, Eric got up.

'I suppose,' he said, 'after proving myself such a poor watchman, I'd better check my sister's room first.'

With that, he left me to go upstairs. It was seconds later that I heard him calling Martha's name.

Then he called mine.

I met Eric at the top of the stairs.

'Martha's not in her room. I've checked the bathroom. I've checked all the rooms up here. She must have let herself out. The key's still on the inside of her bedroom door.'

I was worried, but didn't want Eric to see it.

'Maybe,' I said, 'there's another door to the outside, perhaps from the kitchens. Martha might have taken a walk outside. I'll search the rest of the house. You look outside.'

Martha was not in the house. I went outside. Eric was coming towards me, but shaking his head. We met on the courtyard, near the drive which we had used the night before. I saw that there was another, narrower path leading off in a different direction.

Eric saw it at the same time.

'It's the only place I haven't looked,' he said.

I asked him if he wanted to stay behind, but he thought we should go together (18).

16

When I went for the hand cart, it had vanished. I went back to the house to tell Eric and Martha. Martha looked a little better and had actually bandaged Eric's foot and ankle tightly enough for him to be able to hobble on it. Cart or no cart, Eric was now determined to leave.

Near the driveway was a second, narrower path which looked as if it might be a short cut to the road. With the thought of saving Eric's ankle, we took it.

Not far down the path, we smelled burning and could see smoke drifting across the path. Curiosity aroused, Eric pushed his way through the trees towards it.

We followed him, entering a small clearing with a wide stream at the bottom of it. Beside the stream, stood the cart. Beyond the stream was an old graveyard, overgrown with thorn and ivy and looking as though it had been undisturbed for centuries.

The smoke came from what remained of an ancient oak tree in the graveyard – a victim of the night's storm. The gnarled trunk was split apart and still smouldered at its centre. Beside it was a mound of fresh earth, as if the bolt of lightning which had struck the tree had also scooped a great hole from the ground.

Eric went up to the cart and then walked a little way both up and down stream.

'That's odd,' he said. 'The graveyard's an island. I can see the stream running down both sides of it. Why is there no bridge? But no matter. We wanted the cart. We've found it!'

'We can't take it now,' said Martha. 'Obviously someone is using it.'

'Well, there's no-one here – and it is only an old wreck,' Eric insisted. 'After just that walk from the house, I can tell you I'll not get to Valdah unless I can ride some of the way. I'll bring it back, if that'll make you happier.'

Martha wasn't happy and the argument went on. I was looking at the opposite bank of the stream. In the mud were footprints, one tiny, the other with a distinctive pattern, identical with a walking shoe owned by Martha! I didn't want her to see it. I had to get them away quickly – by siding with Eric (**21**), or Martha (**17**).

17

If Martha Hoffman had been to the deserted graveyard during the night, then why had she gone and who had taken her? I was sure that Martha remembered nothing, yet I had the same sense of an evil presence that I had felt in the house. The cart was a part of it and I wanted to leave it all behind as quickly as possible.

'Martha is right,' I said. 'Someone is using the cart. They may have every right to do so. We are strangers in a foreign land. I have heard of people being jailed for less than stealing a cart. We'll walk. We can cut you a stick, Eric, to help you along.'

As we left the clearing, we saw a man standing watching us from the trees. He was dressed in the long coat and hat of a priest.

'They call it "The Vampires' Graveyard",' he said. 'Don't worry! They have rested here for more than three centuries, each pinned to the ground with a sharp stake of wood through its heart. The water is an extra precaution. The river was diverted so that the graveyard would be surrounded. Vampires cannot cross water – but enough of that! I am Father Sebastian from Valdah. The lights in the old house caused a sensation in my village last night. I thought you more likely to be lost travellers than vampires and I came looking for you. My car is a little way off.'

The priest's car was more of a surprise than the priest. A 'twenties' Hispano-Suiza, he explained that it had been left with him during the war and never collected. The bodywork was lovingly kept. The engine did not appear to have had the same attention.

Father Sebastian explained that the whole secret lay in 'the choke', though he had not yet worked out exactly what the secret was.

It took thirty minutes to get the car started. Eric and Martha were seated in the seclusion of the hooded rear of the car, while I sat up front with Father Sebastian.

At last we began our journey to Valdah at a steady thirty kilometres an hour (**22**).

18

We had not walked far along the path before we smelled burning and saw smoke drifting across from between the trees. It seemed too wet for anything still to be burning from the storm of the night before. Perhaps someone was camping and Martha had already found them.

A few paces beyond the path, the trees opened out into a small clearing. At the bottom of the clearing was a wide stream and, beyond it, an old graveyard. It was completely overgrown with thorn and ivy and looked as if it had been undisturbed for centuries. The smoke came from what remained of an ancient oak tree a victim of the night's storm. Its branches lay, broken, around it. The gnarled trunk was split apart and still smouldered at its centre. Beside it was a heap of fresh earth, as if the bolt of lightning which had struck the tree had also scooped a great hole from the ground.

Eric had moved nearer and now began to walk up and down the length of the bank of the stream.

'It's an island!' he called, 'yet there seems no way across; no bridge or any sign of there ever having been one.'

I had also moved closer. I was looking at the mud bank on the opposite side of the stream. In it were two sets of footprints, one tiny, the other of a walking shoe with a very distinctive pattern. Martha Hoffman owned such a pair. Only a short distance away in long grass I found Martha's unconscious body. Her clothes were drenched, her skin almost white and I could hardly feel her pulse.

Eric wrapped her in his coat and we carried her back towards the house. As we crossed the courtyard, Eric caught his foot in a broken stone, badly twisting his ankle. So it was with the greatest difficulty, that we carried Martha into the house. I wanted to get her up to bed, but Eric wasn't sure he could manage the stairs.

Then, from outside, came what sounded for all the world like a very old motor car. A figure appeared silhouetted in the outer doorway. All I could make out was a long cloak or coat and a hat of a shape usually worn by a priest.

'I,' he said, 'am Father Sebastian from Valdah.'

(19)

19

He stepped straight over to Martha who was sitting with her eyes open, but seemed hardly aware of the priest's arrival. I saw him looking at her neck and noticed, for the first time, that there were two small marks with spots of blood on them. Perhaps thinking we would not see while his back was towards us, he crossed himself.

'This girl . . .'

'Martha Hoffman, my sister,' Eric prompted.

'Your sister could be in need of medical attention. I suggest you build up the fire and try to keep her warm.'

'Eric has twisted his ankle,' I said. 'I will do what I can, but I wonder if we should try to get her up to bed.'

'No!' The answer was very definite. 'You must leave this house!'

'What's wrong with the house?' Eric asked as I put more logs on the fire, 'and for that matter, why are you here?'

'I am here because lights were seen in the house last night from my village. There have been no lights here for ten years. I guessed you might be stranded travellers. As to what is wrong with the house, that is a long and unpleasant story.'

'But all these treasures?' Eric queried.

'Safer than you think. Only I would venture near the place – and it does have a caretaker. You will not have seen him. He has good reason for not wanting to be seen. But enough questions. When the girl is a little recovered, believe me that she must be taken from here.'

'To Valdah?' Eric asked.

'I can take you to Valdah, but there is no doctor. The nearest is in Chesku, the next village, but the roads are flooded and there is no way he can get through. I can try to get you to Sabrov. There is a hospital there.'

'Then it must be Sabrov,' Eric replied.

'Wait!' said Father Sebastian. 'I said I could try. One road is open. In times of heavy rain there are often landslides. I'm afraid the age of my car would make the journey doubly dangerous.'

Eric looked at me. 'Help me,' he said. 'Valdah (**22**), or Sabrov (**24**)?'

20

I had thought nothing had happened during the night. Then I remembered Martha's appearance and her wet clothes. Something surely had happened, something which I found disturbing and frightening.

When I had left the house, I had felt that I might be leaving Eric and Martha in some unknown danger. Perhaps the danger was, for the moment, over, but somehow, I knew that Martha Hoffman was already involved in it.

I must have left the clearing by a different route from the one I had come by. Barring my way was a hand cart, the wood badly charred. Surely it was the one from the house! Lying on it was a long box. It was the size of a coffin, but I told myself that it was nothing more than a packing case. I had no idea of its purpose, or why it was there. I pushed the cart out of the way. As I did so, the box slid off and the lid opened!

It took me some time to bring myself to look inside. The box contained only a layer of soil, soil which had pieces of charred wood among it.

I left the box on the ground and hurried on to

the house.

Eric and Martha were clearly surprised to see me back so soon. I wasn't really certain what to tell them, but Eric half saved the day by showing me that Martha had bound his foot and ankle up and that now he could hobble about on it.

I noticed that as Martha got up from bandaging Eric's foot, she was having to hold onto the chair to steady herself. I helped her over to one of the other chairs where she was grateful just to sit. Though the day was warm, her skin was ice cold and I could hardly feel the pulse in her wrist where I had been holding it.

I was waiting for them to ask why I had come back so quickly, when the air was shattered by the bang and clatter of what had to be a very old motor car, out in the courtyard.

We turned to watch the open doorway. A figure appeared in it, silhouetted against the light. All I could make out was a long, dark cloak or coat and a hat of a shape usually worn by a priest.

'I,' he said, 'am Father Sebastian from Valdah.'
(19)

21

The cart had two wheels, a flat top and a long handle which could be pushed or pulled. I began to push it out of the clearing.

'I will need a hand to get it through the trees and onto the pathway,' I said. 'I expect you, Eric, to walk for as long as you can. The cart is heavy. With you on it, it will be even heavier.'

The path did meet the main road and Eric lasted the better part of three of the five kilometres before his ankle gave out. With Eric on the cart and Martha and me pushing, we covered another kilometre. Suddenly, I felt a strain on the handle. Martha was no longer pushing. She was lying on the road in a dead faint!

Eric got down. Together, we got Martha onto the cart. If I could push, Eric thought he could hobble the rest of the way. It cound not be far.

Valdah was the picture-book village, its decorated timber buildings looking as if they had remained unchanged for centuries. We must have looked a little strange as we entered the main street since people seemed to be moving quickly away from us. I heard a woman shout, 'It's the fiend's cart!' as she shut herself in her house. A group of men stood staring at us.

'We need help,' I said. 'Can't you see we need help! The girl is ill. My friend is injured.'

The men did not move.

'They have come from the house,' one of them said. 'Now do you believe that I saw lights last night?'

'It *is* the fiend's cart,' said another '– but the other one – he can't have returned. We destroyed him ten years ago. I was there. I saw it!'

I was beginning to feel desperate when a gentle touch on my shoulder made me stop. The man beside me wore the long coat and hat of a priest.

'I am Father Sebastian,' he said. 'This is my house beside the church. I will help you get the cart into the courtyard.'

As we were taking Martha into the priest's house. I turned to see the cart vanishing through a side door in the courtyard wall. Even though Martha was now in good hands, I wanted to stay to help her (**28**). I also knew it was the cart, not us that the villagers feared – I wanted to know who had spirited it away so quickly, and why (**23**).

22

Valdah was the picture-book village, its decorated, timbered buildings looking as if they had remained unchanged for centuries. While Father Sebastian sat at the wheel of the car, I had the job of shooing ducks and geese from its path. As we moved down the main street, there was a lot of shouting and we could see that a crowd had gathered outside the church.

Father Sebastian stopped the car.

'Stay here,' he said, and walked towards the crowd which parted as he approached. Now we could see a dwarf of a man being kicked and struck as he lay on the ground.

'Stop!'

At the priest's voice, the crowd stood back. He walked over and helped the dwarf to his feet. As he did so, the tiny man turned to face us. I felt suddenly, sick. One side of the man's face was terribly scarred and burned. He tried to cover it with his left hand; a hand that had on it a thumb and the stumps of three fingers.

'He was in the church!' someone shouted. 'The fiend was in the church!'

'Is not the church open to all?' asked the priest.

'If his appearance is that of a fiend, then some of you might ask yourselves why it is so; or is it that your memories are short?'

There was a sudden silence, then a murmuring among the crowd as they began to drift away. The dwarf moved towards the car. It was obvious to anyone that he was hurt. Blood streamed over his ghastly features and he walked as if in great pain.

Father Sebastian came back.

'You wonder why I do not offer him help. He could not accept it from me. I represent, to him, another world, a threat to all he believes in.'

I looked back at Eric and Martha. Martha had fainted, perhaps from shock. Eric seemed unable to revive her. The priest looked at her more closely. The two marks on her neck, which I took to be insect bites, were bleeding.

'The girl is ill,' said the priest. 'Her brother and I will see to her needs. My advice is to forget what you have seen and come with us (28). But you must follow your conscience. If you want to help the dwarf, his name is Toomis. There is a first aid box in the car.'(25)

23

I thought that my absence for a few moments might hardly be noticed. I slipped through the doorway in the courtyard wall and found myself in a narrow lane which ran between the priest's house and the church. The cart was not in sight.

I reached a turning in the lane and stopped, first peering cautiously around the corner. The lane ended at a low door in the wall of the church. There was the cart and there, fitting a key into the lock of the door, was a man so small I could only describe him as a dwarf.

I watched as he unlocked the door, pushed it open and then turned back towards the cart. I pulled back my head so that he didn't see me, but not before I had seen something that made me feel sick to the pit of my stomach.

The left side of the man's face was terribly burned and scarred. Above his right eye was a gash from which blood poured. He tried to wipe it away with his left hand – a hand with only a thumb and the stumps of three fingers!

I heard the cart bumping down stone stairs, then, a sudden crash and a cry of pain. I took a very deep breath and ran to the door. In the half darkness at the bottom of the stairs, I could see the dwarf with the cart on top of him. I ran down the stairs.

'My 'eg!' he said, ' 's stuck 'n the whee'f the cart. I can't 'ift. Is too heavy.'

He spoke oddly through a twisted mouth, but the message was clear. I lifted the cart while he drew out his leg.

' 's not broken,' he said, feeling it.

I gave him my handkerchief to staunch the blood above his eye.

'You no' frighten of me.'

'No,' I said. 'You're face isn't pretty, but you can't help that. If we had some light, I might do a better job of patching you up.'

I looked round the room. I thought it must be the crypt of the church. Dark though it was, it looked empty except for a long packing case, almost like a coffin! I was wondering what it was when the dwarf said, 'No ques'ions. If you my friend you haven' see me. Go back to priest's house.' **(28)**

24

Martha seemed to make a slight recovery in front of the fire. Father Sebastian was in a great hurry to leave and was sure she was fit enough to be helped out to the car.

The car was just another surprise. It was a Hispano-Suiza, one of the luxury cars of the twenties! The body was brown and orange and it had a brown leather hood which completely covered the passenger seats at the back. The bodywork had been lovingly kept. From the sound it had made as it approached the house, the same could not be said of the engine!

With Eric and Martha in the back, I waited for Father Sebastian to get into the driving seat. Instead, he turned to me.

'Would you like to drive?'

I said that I'd never driven such a car.

'I'm afraid you'll have to,' he said. 'It's my eyesight. I never drive at more than thirty kilometres an hour. The road we are taking is often steep and winding and I am not very good at finding the right gears.'

The car was not difficult to drive and livelier than I expected. By the time we came to the steeper part of the road to Sabrov, I was feeling confident.

I had reached a section of road which was reasonably flat, but narrow and curved sharply around the hillside.

On one side was a sheer drop. On the other, trees climbed the steep hillside.

The rattle of a few stones on the road in front of me made me look up the hill. The trees were moving! Father Sebastian followed my gaze.

'It's all the water from the storms,' he said, almost casually. 'It's a landslide.'

More stones were coming down. I couldn't both watch the road and the trees. In my mind, I could see us being completely buried under tons of earth at any second!

'What do I do?' I shouted. I knew Eric and Martha would not be able to see what was happening for the hood. I was looking at the priest.

'Turn back to Valdah now,' he said, 'and I think we will be safe.' (22) 'If you go on, I will pray – and you might find it helpful to give the car a little more choke.' (26)

25

I watched Martha being carried into the priest's house, before I took the first aid box and followed Toomis who was now some distance away. As he heard me running towards him, he half turned, then stopped.

'You' not fro' the village,' he said. His mouth was scarred and twisted and his speech slurred. 'You was at the house 'ast night.'

'Yes,' I said. 'I came to see what I could do for your cuts.'

'Can you stop blood 'bove a right eye? I got only a right eye. They burned me – but I 'scape. Frighten of me. You no' frighten of me?'

'No,' I answered. 'Your face is not pretty, but you can't help that. You've been badly burned.'

'I 'ook after house for master's return. Clean it. No' easy.'

He held up the stumps of his fingers.

' 'Ast night, he is free by storm. Tonight he come back to house.'

He pointed to the village.

'Then they have reason to be frighten of poor Toomis!'

'That's the best I can do.' I said.

There were no thanks. Toomis just walked away. He did stop to call back, 'I tell master you my friend.'

I returned to the priest's house. Martha had been taken upstairs and put to bed by Margheta, Father Sebastian's housekeeper. The priest himself was doing a fine strapping job on Eric's ankle.

'The road to Chesku is still flooded,' the priest explained, 'so we have no doctor. Don't worry. Margheta knows what to do in these cases.'

He spoke as if he knew exactly what ailed Martha but, before I could ask, he was asking me how I had got on with Toomis.

I told him I thought the poor creature a little mad, but probably harmless. I repeated what he had said about the return of the master and how he had been 'freed' by the storm.

Father Sebastian stopped his work on Eric's ankle.

'Last night was Koljada, the night when the dead return. I did not want to believe it – but still, he cannot leave the graveyard.' **(29)**

26

I pulled on the choke and put my foot to the floor on the accelerator. The car leapt forward. Earth was coming down on top of us like black rain and I could hardly keep the car on the bend through the mud piling in front of us. There was a great crash as, somewhere, close behind us, the first of the trees had reached the road. Martha had begun to scream and my arms felt about to tear from their sockets as I strained, desperately, to hold the wheel.

Suddenly, the road was clear! I eased off the accelerator and stopped the car. Behind us, it was as if no road had ever been there, only a continuous slope of earth and broken trees, still sliding gently downwards.

'There's Sabrov,' said Father Sebastian, pointing. 'We'll be there in a short while.' Then, as an aside, he added, 'I must use that choke more often myself.'

We reached Sabrov, and the hospital. Eric went along with his sister and Father Sebastian and I waited. Two hours later Eric returned with one of the doctors. I noticed that Eric had had his ankle properly strapped and was walking with only the slightest limp.

'How's Martha?' I asked.

'She will be fine,' the doctor replied. He started to smile. 'I gather this happened near Valdah which I suppose you know is the very heart of Romania's vampire country. I'm sorry to have to disappoint you about the two marks on her neck. There were several more on her body. I would say they were caused by a blood sucking insect. Some people react very badly to insect bites. Miss Hoffman is one of them and really must keep out of forests during hot, wet summers.'

Father Sebastian would take no reward for his kindness and decided to visit an old friend in Sabrov until the road to Valdah had been cleared. Martha came out of hospital two days later and the three of us travelled to Constanta by rail. With only three days left before we were due to fly home, and with Martha still a little weak, we chose to spend the time in one of Constanta's luxury hotels.

On our last night, Martha had gone to bed and I was sitting with Eric in the hotel lounge (**27**).

27

'Martha is either unable, or unwilling to remember exactly what happened to her the night we spent in that house,' Eric told me, 'and this is the first chance I have had to ask you what the priest told you. Please satisfy my curiosity!'

Father Sebastian had not said a great deal. He seemed reluctant to talk about it, but he had told me a little.

In the seventeenth century, Valdah had been made famous by a monk who had published a small tract called *The Vampyres of Valdah*. So much had the village been plagued by these demon creatures that a priest from Rome had been sent to deal with the matter. All those suspected of having any connection with these creatures of Hell were put to death. They and the bodies of those already believed to be vampires were duly buried in a small graveyard with the traditional stake driven through their hearts. As an added precaution, a local river was diverted so that the graveyard would be surrounded by water. Vampires cannot cross water.

Among those put to death was the whole household of the house where we stayed. Not surprisingly, it remained empty until ten years ago when it was bought by a rich, eccentric stranger, Count Sorza, who lived alone with only one servant, a dwarf called Toomis.

'Then, after a number of mysterious deaths among young women in the village, I suppose hysteria broke out. The whole village descended on the house and set fire to it. The Count died in the blaze. Toomis tried to escape, but was caught, tied to a cart, tar poured over him and set ablaze. By some miracle, he lived. Father Sebastian says the poor, deformed creature is now half mad, but keeps the house as best he can, believing his master will return from the dead.

'I must admit,' I added. 'It's quite a story!'

Eric handed me the evening paper and pointed to a small paragraph, 'Mystery Epidemic Strikes Isolated Village. Reports reaching us from Valdah, presently cut off by floods and landslides, tell of several mysterious and unaccountable deaths among young women in the village. A team of medical experts are, today, flying in from the capital to investigate.'

28

Martha had been put to bed and was being looked after by Margheta, Father Sebastian's housekeeper. Father Sebastian himself was doing a fine job of strapping up Eric's ankle.

'The road to Chesku is still flooded,' the priest explained, 'so we have no doctor. There is no need to worry. Margheta knows what to do.'

It was at that moment that Margheta appeared.

'I've made her comfortable, Father,' she said, and then added something which I was certain I was not meant to overhear – 'She has the marks, Father!'

Perhaps thinking that I had overheard, Father Sebastian quickly changed the subject.

'You will know that Toomis, the dwarf has been in trouble in the village again.'

'Know!' Margheta replied. 'I was there when he came out of the church. I didn't agree with the way they treated him, but I was hardly surprised after the things he was shouting.'

'Toomis,' Father Sebastian told Eric and me, 'is the caretaker of the house you spent the night in. He is a little odd in the head; though that's not surprising after what happened to him. He keeps the place for the return of his master – who died ten years ago.'

'Not according to Toomis; not any more, that is,' Margheta interrupted.

Father Sebastian stopped his work on Eric's leg and looked at Margheta.

'It's the truth I'm telling, Father. I can't remember the dwarf's exact words. I think he said that his master had been released by the storm and would soon be back in the house. It has to be true. How else do you account for the girl upstairs?'

'There must be some other explanation,' the priest replied. 'Last night was Koljada. Toomis knows that as well as we do.'

'What is "Koljada"?' I asked.

'An old superstition,' the priest answered. 'It is supposed to be the night when the dead return. I'm afraid that we are still very superstitious people.'

Then he murmured to himself, 'It cannot be possible. At least there is no way that he can leave the graveyard.' **(29)**

29

Father Sebastian turned back to finish the job of strapping up Eric's ankle.

'I suppose,' he said, to Eric and myself, 'that you know nothing of the history of Valdah or the house where you spent the night.'

Seeing our agreement, he went on.

'Valdah was made famous in the seventeenth century by the monk, Sestis, who published a small tract called *The Vampyres of Valdah*. He recounts how the village was plagued by these demons and how many young women died through having the blood sucked from them while they slept. So terrible was it that a priest was sent from Rome – an expert in such matters.

'He declared that the demons were in league with a powerful family who lived in the house where you stayed and, as it happened, were also enemies of Rome! He had them put to death. They and the bodies of those believed to be vampires were then buried in the small graveyard which lies on the edge of the wood below the house. Each corpse had a stake driven through its heart and, as a further precaution, a local river was diverted so that the graveyard became an island.

Vampires cannot cross water.

'The house remained empty and ruined until ten years ago when it was bought by a rich, eccentric stranger, Count Sorza, who lived alone with only one servant, a dwarf called Toomis.

'Then a number of mysterious deaths took place among young girls in the village. One night, what I can only describe as "mass hysteria" broke out. The whole village descended on the house and set fire to it. The Count died in the fire. Toomis escaped, was caught, tied to a cart, tar was poured over him and set on fire. By some miracle, he survived. Since then, he has kept the house and its treasures, awaiting the return of his dead master.'

'Are you telling us that the Count has returned and that my sister has been attacked by a vampire?' Eric asked.

Father Sebastian laughed.

'The thought did cross my mind, but I suspect that your sister is suffering from some insect bite. Your ankle is done, and now I am due in church – and if you visit the church, don't go into the crypt. It's dangerous – woodworm!' **(30)**

30

Eric and I visited Martha in her bedroom. She was still pale, but awake and looking greatly recovered – sufficiently so to be able to joke with us.

'Margheta,' she said, 'is a dear, kind woman, but she's living in the dark ages! She thinks that I've been attacked by a vampire!'

'It's the marks on your neck,' Eric said.

'Insect bites,' Martha replied. 'They do something to me. I've had a bad time with them before – but have you seen this room; or smelt it for that matter!'

I had noticed that the room had been hung with wild garlic around both the door and the windows.

'She wanted to hang it round my neck – vampires don't like garlic! That reminds me; I've lost my little gold cross and chain. It could have come off anywhere – a pity. I was very fond of it.'

Eric spent much of the day with his sister, at the same time resting his ankle. I walked around the village, then spent the rest of the day in the priest's library trying to find information on vampires. I found nothing.

By night time, the storm was back, though

without the same fury as the night before. Martha was asleep. Eric was sure that vampires were just a myth but, in case he was wrong, he intended to keep a careful watch on his sister through the night.

I hadn't seen Father Sebastian since supper and asked Margheta if he was in the house. She replied only that he was out. It seemed late for him to be out and I could see that Margheta was worried. I pressed her to tell me where the priest had gone.

'I'm not certain,' she said, 'but he took a spade and lantern with him and told me to say nothing.'

'Is he walking?' I asked.

She nodded. Apparently the lights on the priest's car did not work.

I could guess as well as Margheta where he'd gone! It was a terrible night to be out and I was not certain I could find my way to the graveyard in the dark. But Father Sebastian was not telling us everything and one way of learning the rest would be to follow him (34). On the other hand, if Martha was in danger, someone should be here and awake! (32)

31

'The person who told me is long dead,' the priest continued, 'so that only I knew the secret.'

I was still reluctant to accept the idea. This was the twentieth century!

'The lightning,' I said. 'Surely the lightning has destroyed the body!'

The priest shook his head.

'Not so completely,' he answered. 'There is nothing down there but earth and charred wood. I too find it hard to accept that we have a vampire in Valdah!'

As he spoke, the stone cross beside him began very slowly to tilt. I shouted a warning. The priest sprang back. The cross leaned slowly towards the hole – and then stopped.

'The digging and the rain!' said Father Sebastian, ' – but no harm done. If it falls, we can do little about it, and we have more important tasks. The girl, Martha Hoffman, is certainly in danger. You must return to my house and help her brother keep watch over her.'

'Will you return with me?' I asked.

'Not yet,' he answered. 'There are other things

which I must do. Now go, quickly.'

I found my way back to the road. The storm was easing, but the darker sky made my return more slow and difficult.

At last, I entered the main street of Valdah. The rain had stopped and the sky was clearing. I made my way to the priest's house. As I neared it there was a movement somewhere in the deeper shadows.

'You're 'fraid for the girl!'

Toomis, the dwarf was standing in front of me.

'I said you 'fraid for the girl!'

'What if I am?' I answered him.

'Toomis can he' –'

His twisted mouth gave him difficulty with the word.

'How can you help?' I asked.

'You mus' come wi' Toomis. Come now!'

Had I any reason to trust the dwarf? Perhaps he could help. Martha was already in danger. Could I too be putting myself at risk? Should I go with him (36), or refuse his offer (38)?

32

Eric had been given a room directly across the corridor from Martha's. I went upstairs to see if all was well. Eric's door was open and I could see him seated, reading in a chair. I went in.

I asked him whether he intended to go to bed or to sit in the chair all night. He said that he was certainly not going to bed. He hoped to manage to stay awake seated in the chair.

Remembering our experiences of the night before I thought that, if left alone, neither of us was good at staying awake. Perhaps the only thing I could do was to stay with Eric, talking, or finding some other way to pass the time so that we might keep each other from falling asleep.

Eric was grateful for the offer. An hour had passed and Margheta had gone to her room, when there was an urgent knocking on the front door. Knowing that Margheta was probably in her bed and might take some time to answer it, I took one of the two oil lamps from Eric's room and went downstairs. A man stood outside in the courtyard, well muffled against the storm, but he was someone I was sure I did not recognise.

'Is the priest in his bed?' he asked.

I told him that Father Sebastian had gone out earlier in the evening and had not returned.

'Then there is nothing to do,' the man said, 'but leave a message for his return.'

I said that I would gladly pass the message on.

'Tell him that the old dam has broken and that the river runs its old course. There has been no water there for centuries and houses were built on the old river bed. Some have been washed away and many people may be hurt. I thought that the priest should know.'

As he turned to leave, I asked him, 'Is that the dam which was built to surround the vampires' graveyard with water?'

For a moment, he hesitated, surprised maybe at such a question from a stranger to the village.

'What other dam might there be?' he grunted, turned on his heel, and was gone. I wondered again whether I should follow the priest to the graveyard (**34**), or help Eric keep his vigil (**33**).

33

As I closed the door, I heard Margheta's footsteps on the stairs behind me. She asked who it was at this late hour. I said I didn't know the man, but told her the message which he had left.

'Then it's happened!' she said, 'just as the dwarf told it.'

Margheta knew all about Toomis's visit to the village that day and his boast about his master being released by the storm, and soon returning to the house. This news had visibly shaken her.

'Your friend tells me that the two of you intend to keep watch over the girl through the night. I will make you something to drink and some food to help you stay awake.'

I said that there was no need for her to go to such trouble, but she insisted, saying that if she went back to her own bed now, she was sure she wouldn't sleep.

I followed her to the kitchen.

'Tell me about vampires,' I asked her. 'I know that they can wander abroad only in the hours of darkness, and at sunrise they have to return to their graves.'

Margheta nodded.

'So if there is a vampire, he must return to the graveyard at dawn?'

'It could be,' Margheta replied, spreading butter on bread, 'but it could be to some other place which the dwarf has prepared. It need only be a box lined with earth from the grave. Such a box could be hidden anywhere.'

'And how could it be found?' I asked her.

This time, she shook her head.

'There is no certain way – and there could be more than one box in which the vampire could rest through the hours of daylight.'

Margheta made the task of finding such boxes seem almost impossible. She was probably right!

She had finished making the sandwiches and had heated up some milk. I wanted to talk to her more, but offered to take Eric's upstairs to him.

I had promised Eric that I would help him keep watch through the night (37), but a thought was forming at the back of my mind. What had Toomis been doing in the church? It was only next door the the priest's house! (35)

34

Margheta had found me another lantern, but I was most grateful for the storm. Without the flicker of lightning in the sky, I would never have found my way along the road through the forest. As I thought I was nearing the house, I struck off hopefully through the trees. There it was – the light of another lantern! I made my way towards it.

As I got nearer, I called out, 'Father Sebastian!'

The priest's voice came back.

'I thought you might follow me. Margheta has never been known to keep a secret and I judged you were curious enough to brave the night and the storm. Watch where you tread. The river which made this place an island, is gone. The old dam which was used to change its course must have broken.'

I struggled through the mud which had been the stream bed and I was in the graveyard. The sight which met my eyes was enough to make anyone believe in demons.

The priest stood, resting on his spade. On his left, the lantern hung on the broken branch of an oak tree, blasted by lightning. On his right was a tall stone cross. The whole scene was starkly lit by a sky suddenly ripped apart by flashes of light. The gusting wind moaned through the trees like the rise and fall of the unearthly murmurings of a thousand voices.

'Come no farther,' the priest said. 'There is a deep hole in front of you. The lightning which struck that tree had done most of the work for me, but I have dug deeper to be quite certain.'

'Certain of what?' I asked.

'Certain of what I most feared. The dwarf was telling the truth. I told you that Count Sorza died in the fire. I did not tell you that the body was buried here with a stake of wood through its heart. I had no part in it. I did not believe in such superstition – though, perhaps, even in those days I had doubts. Now, I must believe. The grave is empty.'

'Toomis, the dwarf,' I said, 'could he not have dug up the body?'

'No. Only one person knew where it was buried. It was told to me under the seal of confession.' **(31)**

35

From my explorations earlier the previous day, I knew that there were two entrances to the church crypt, one from within the church itself, the other by way of an outside door in the alley beyond the courtyard of the priest's house.

I asked Margheta if there was a key to the crypt. She reluctantly gave me the key to the outside door. She also gave me a lantern.

I was surprised to find the outside door to the crypt already unlocked. I pushed it open and held up the lantern. I could see nothing but the stone steps going down to the crypt.

I walked, slowly, down the steps, stopping at the bottom to look about me. The place appeared to be completely empty and deserted. I heard the outer door close with an echoing clash but, before I could turn back up the stairs, a shape had emerged from the deeper shadows. Thinking it might be Toomis, I lifted the lantern higher. The light fell upon a face with fine, classical, strangely handsome features.

'I,' said the stranger, 'am Count Sorza.'

I looked, desperately, about me, wondering

where I might find the other exit to the church.

'There is no way out,' the Count continued in a quiet, cultured voice. 'There is no way out except upon my terms. You know too much for me to let you go freely from here; but I am a civilised man and I will offer you a choice.'

Another light appeared as Toomis approached from the darkness carrying an oil lamp. He stopped a little way from his master. The Count looked neither old, nor young. There was an ageless quality about both his face and figure. His appearance was, in no way frightening. I felt that the same might not be true of the 'choice' which he was about to offer.

'If it is your wish,' he said, 'I will give you a quick and Christian death. I hope you will take the other choice. I have the power to make you like myself.'

'A vampire!' I exclaimed.

'I do not find that a distasteful word,' the Count replied. 'What I am offering you is eternal life!'
(39)

36

The dwarf led me up the side alley between the priest's house and the church. From my explorations earlier in the day, I knew that it led to the outside door of the crypt.

When I had left in such haste for the graveyard, Margheta had given me some keys on a string, one of them to let myself back into the house. I had noticed that it also held some keys to the church, including the outside door to the crypt; or so said its neatly printed label. I felt better for having it. I could not trust Toomis completely and had no intention of being locked in the crypt!

When we reached the crypt door, it was not locked. Toomis pushed it open.

'You go down 'e stairs. I fo'ow you.'

I walked slowly down the steps, stopping at the bottom. The place appeared deserted. I heard the outer door close with a clash but, before I had time to look up the stairs, a shape had emerged from the deeper shadows. The light of my lantern fell upon a face with fine, classical, strangely handsome features.

'I,' said the stranger, 'am Count Sorza.'

I looked, desperately, about me, wondering where I might find the other exit to the church.

'There is no way out,' the Count continued in a quiet, cultured voice. 'There is no way out except upon my terms. You know too much for me to let you go freely from here, but I am a civilised man and I will offer you a choice.'

Another light appeared as Toomis approached from the darkness carrying an oil lamp. He stopped a little way from his master. The Count looked neither old, nor young. There was an ageless quality about both his face and figure. His appearance was in no way frightening. I felt that the same might not be true of the 'choice' which he was about to offer.

'If it is your wish,' he said, 'I will give you a quick and Christian death. I hope you will take the other choice. I have the power to make you like myself.'

'A vampire!' I exclaimed.

'I do not find that a distasteful word,' the Count replied. 'What I am offering you is eternal life!'
(39)

37

It was now the early hours of morning. The storm had died down, the rain had stopped and the sky was clearing. Eric had begun to nod off yet again and I was running out of conversation. I leant over and shook him by the shoulder.

'Sorry!' he said. 'I'm glad I have you with me. I don't know how you are able to stay awake!'

'With difficulty!' I told him. 'Perhaps the cold draught on my feet is helping.'

As I said it, I realised that while the draught was real enough, I couldn't remember feeling it for more than the past few minutes. It was as if a door or window had been opened suddenly. Eric looked at me.

'Have you heard something?' he asked, anxiously.

'No,' I replied. 'It's this draught of cold air. I was wondering where it's coming . . .'

The same thought must have struck us at the same moment. We both picked up our lamps and ran across the corridor to Martha's room. Eric pushed open the door. Martha was lying on the floor. The window was wide open. I closed the window while Eric knelt down beside his sister.

'She's dead!' he gasped. 'I'm sure she's dead!'

I knelt down beside him. Martha looked deathly pale and there was fresh blood on her neck. There was a faint pulse.

'She's not dead,' I said. 'Help me with her onto the bed and I'll get Margheta.'

There was no need to fetch Margheta. She had heard the commotion and appeared in the doorway. She came over to where we had laid Martha on the bed.

'He's been back!' she gasped out, ' – but I put garlic all around the window!'

'No matter,' I answered. 'All that matters now is that he does not come again. Another such visit would surely kill her.'

It was more than an hour till dawn, but I knew that every minute might count. I had to find the resting place of the vampire and destroy him!

The search must begin somewhere; the house to which Toomis had said his master would 're-turn' (**41**), or the church crypt which was 'unsafe' to visit (**35**).

38

Suddenly, from the priest's house, I heard Eric's voice, shouting, and then Margheta's scream. I pushed past the dwarf and made for the courtyard.

Margheta answered my hammering at the door in a state of near hysteria. Eric had found Martha on the floor of her bedroom with fresh blood on her neck and the window of the room open. I rushed up the stairs. Martha lay very white and still on the bed with Eric beside her.

'I didn't go to sleep!' he said, as he saw me. 'I heard nothing. I looked into the room to see if Martha was all right and found her on the floor.'

'It wasn't your fault,' I told him. 'You must stay with your sister. I have no time to explain now, but I must speak to Margheta.

Margheta was crying in the kitchen.

'That poor girl!' she sobbed. 'If that demon comes again tomorrow night, it will surely kill her!'

'Margheta,' I said, 'you must help me. I know little of vampires, but am I right in thinking that they only wander abroad at night?'

She nodded, wiping her eyes on her apron.

'At sunrise, they must return to the earth of their graves.'

'To the graveyard?' I asked.

'It could be,' Margheta replied, 'but it could be to some other place which the dwarf has prepared. It need only be a box lined with earth from the grave. Such a box could be hidden anywhere.'

'Then how could it be found?'

Margheta shook her head.

'That I cannot tell you,' she said. 'There is no way. There could be more than one box of earth in which the vampire could rest.'

Margheta made it sound impossible, but I knew that if Martha's life was to be saved, then every minute might count. It was still dark and more than an hour till dawn, but I had to start looking. I could think of one possible place; the strange house in which we had spent the night – the house to which Toomis claimed his master would 'return' (41). One other thought entered my mind. What had Toomis been doing in the church; the church with a crypt where no-one went because it was unsafe (35)?

39

'You find that a difficult idea, perhaps,' the Count continued. 'I was not always known by the name of Count Sorza. I have had many names in my time. In the courts of the Pharaohs, I was Mycenos. The Greeks knew me as Philias, the Romans, as Sextus. I have lived through the history of this world, seen the burning of the great library at Alexandria, watched Hannibal's crossing of the Alps, entered Moscow with the armies of Napoleon.'

I could not deny that the offer had about it a terrible fascination, but I knew that the price was too high. I could think of nothing but to stall for time so that I might find some way of escaping.

'If I were to accept this offer,' I said, 'then what of my friend Martha Hoffman? Would the girl's life be safe?'

The Count looked at me, I thought almost with pity.

'I wonder,' he said, 'whether you are ready for what I offer you. Now, you see this girl, Martha Hoffman as your friend. As one of us, you would see her as just another mere mortal, a small sacrifice for a life which is eternal. Vampires do not have friends. Friends grow old and die. We do not.'

Toomis spoke up, at last.

'I am your friend,' he said.

The Count looked at him.

'You are my servant; my good servant.'

'But if I die, wha' wi' you do then?' Toomis asked.

'I will get another servant.'

'But there is no need, Master. You offer eterna' 'ife to this one – who has done nothing for you. Why do you not offer it a'so to me, Toomis who has been fai'fu' to you for many years?'

For a moment, the Count was silent.

'I do not offer it because you are what you are, an ugly dwarf who has served me well in return for the rewards which I have given you. That is how it will remain until the end of your days. Eternity is not for the likes of you.'

Toomis's already twisted face now took on an expression which might have been disappointment, or anger (**45**).

40

I ran through the thorns behind the priest and around the other side of the open grave. I dared not look towards the priest and vampire. I felt sure that once caught in the vampire's gaze, I would be as helpless as Father Sebastian.

I reached the leaning marble cross and, with all the strength that was in me, I began to push. I felt the stone move. Again I tried. It moved again, and then began to slip away from me. It was falling into the grave! As it fell I threw the tiny cross and chain beneath it. Unless the vampire's will could move a ton of solid marble, there was no way the cross could be taken from the grave.

Suddenly, I was conscious that the Count was beside me. I looked at his face. It was no longer handsome, but twisted in an expression of unutterable fury. His mouth had begun to move as the first rays of the rising sun fell full upon him. He raised his arms to cover his face. For a moment, he held them there. They fell, suddenly, to his sides. There was no longer a face behind them; only a crumbling mask of rotting flesh and decaying bone. Slowly, the whole figure collapsed in front of me until it was no more than a heap of grey dust at my feet. As I watched, the dust was lifted away by the morning breeze.

Everything else had gone from my mind. I just stood, staring – numbed, revolted, speechless. An arm was placed gently around my shoulders.

'The task was well done.'

The gentle voice was Father Sebastian's. I looked up, not knowing how I expected him to appear.

'I am almost recovered,' he said, 'in body, if not in spirit. I think that we two should now leave this place – you the wiser, and I the humbler.'

Father Sebastian would not talk about what had happened at the house that night before I reached the graveyard. Toomis left the district on the following day and, that night, what remained of the house, together with its treasures, was totally destroyed by a mysterious fire.

A week later, Martha Hoffman was well enough to leave Valdah. I still write to Martha and Eric but we no longer spend our summers together.

41

A setting moon now lit the sky and I made good progress along the road to the house. My heart sank when I saw that the house was in total darkness, but I had come this far and I was not turning back until I had once more been through its rooms.

This time, the door of the house was not only unlocked. It was wide open. I thought of calling out to see whether anyone was about, but decided not to advertise my presence.

I found one of the candlesticks we had used the night before. The candles were burned low, but they were still enough to give me the light I needed. As their flames flared up, I saw that something had happened since our leaving. The heavy table at the centre of the room had been overturned. One candlestick lay on the staircase as if it had been suddenly dropped or thrown! I went up the stairs.

The grand, elegant bedroom looked as if a whirlwind had passed through it. The bed linen was on the floor. The bed curtains were torn – and there were traces of fresh blood on them. Surely, there had been a struggle of some kind; I could not guess between whom! There was more blood on the edge of one of the huge tapestries which draped the walls. I pulled it to one side. Behind it was a door – a door which opened onto a narrow, stone staircase that led down through the thickness of the wall.

The stairs seemed never ending, but opened, at last, into the cellars of the house. The air was thick with smoke from the still smouldering remains of a large packing case and earth was strewn across the stone floor. Someone had found and destroyed one of the vampire's possible resting places!

I thought of Father Sebastian. Who else had been in the struggle – Toomis, or Count Sorza himself? Had Father Sebastian already encountered the vampire, and where were they now?

Dawn was only minutes away. If the Count had chosen the house as his resting place, the box was now destroyed. He must seek some other place before the sunrise. There might still be the crypt of the church, but he could never reach it in time. It had to be the graveyard! (43)

42

'Never, priest, is a long time. I do not have that time. In moments, the sun will rise. If I am not then resting in the earth, I am destroyed. Drop the cross!'

The voice had become hard and firm. I looked at Father Sebastian. It was impossible to imagine what the vampire was doing to his mind, but the torment was clear upon his face. I saw the fingers of his hands begin to twitch and blood appear between them as, desperately, he tightened his grip on the cross.

And then it was over. The priest stumbled, fell to his knees, and the cross was on the ground beside him.

'You fought well, priest – but I told you that the battle was unequal. I am sorry that I must now do what has to be done. You know that I must kill you, for if I do not, then you will do as much to me when I am in my grave.'

The vampire was still holding the wooden stake which he had caught. Now with its sharpened end before him, he advanced on the kneeling priest. I waited for Father Sebastian to move. He did not move.

A line of light had appeared just over the horizon. The sun would appear at any second – but it would be too late! I remembered the mallet at my feet. If I could throw it well enough, could I knock the stake from the vampire's hand? If I threw it at the vampire Count himself, could I distract his attention for long enough to give him no time to kill the priest without himself being destroyed?

As I bent down to pick up the mallet, something glistened on the ground beside it. It was a small gold cross and chain. It was surely Martha's gold cross and chain which she had lost.

I held the cross and chain in my hand. I looked at Father Sebastian, still kneeling; a man broken in mind, his cross on the ground before him. In some way, the vampire feared the cross, yet I had seen him break the will of a priest of the church. What hope had I to succeed where Father Sebastian had failed? Time was all but run out. Which should I try to use, the mallet (**44**), or the cross (**40**)?

43

I raced from the house and down towards the edge of the forest. I crossed what was now the dried up river bed and stood at the edge of the graveyard. The first light of dawn was tinging the clouds, though the sun had not yet risen.

On top of a mound of freshly dug earth, stood Father Sebastian, his black clothes standing out against the whitness of the tall, marble cross which was tilted at a rakish angle behind him. In one hand, the priest was holding a wooden stake and a carpenter's mallet. The other hand he held out in front of him. In it, he grasped a large gilt cross of the kind which stands on a church altar.

'You are in my way, priest.'

My eyes turned in the direction of the voice. Standing in the half shadow, was the tall figure of a man. He stepped towards Father Sebastian so that the pale light of the coming dawn fell upon his face. The features were strong, classical, strangely handsome. The voice was soft and cultured.

'You come well prepared, priest, and you have much courage; but the battle is unequal. My will is much stronger than yours.'

Father Sebastian neither answered, nor moved.

'Let me show you, priest. The stake which you hold – the stake which you hope to drive through my heart as I lie helpless in my grave – throw it to me.'

For a moment, nothing happened. Then I saw Father Sebastian's arm move, slowly, as if resisting some invisible force. Suddenly, the stake was flying through the air and the vampire Count had caught it.

'Now, the mallet. Toss it away.'

The mallet landed near my feet. Mercifully for me, the vampire's gaze had not moved from the face of the priest.

'Lastly, the cross. Drop it!'

Even from where I stood, I could see the beads of sweat breaking out on Father Sebastian's forehead. He now grasped the cross with both hands and, in some strange way looked much taller than he had a moment before.

His mouth moved and, carrying with it the anguish of his mind, one word burst from his lips, 'Never!' (42)

44

I threw the mallet at the vampire, knowing as I threw it with my shaking hand that I had no chance of knocking the stake from his grasp. It was only by good fortune that the mallet caught him on the arm which held the stake. I saw the stake fly off into a thicket of thorns.

The Count swung towards me. Instantly, I felt his terrible gaze, as if a numbness were beginning to sieze my mind. I saw his mouth open to speak – and then a sudden brightening in the sky behind him. The vampire too had seen it. Pushing the priest aside he leapt towards the grave.

As he stood at its edge his whole body dissolved into a thin grey mist, vanishing from view as if it were sucked down into the earth.

I looked towards Father Sebastian. He was trying to get up from his knees. I ran to help him. His face was pale, but he managed a weak smile.

'Thank you,' he said, simply. 'And now I must complete the task. There is no need for you to stay.'

I said that I would stay, at least to find the stake and mallet. I did not want to see the rest.

Search as we might, neither could be found.

'It is no use,' said Father Sebastian. 'The stake must be made of oak and it needs tools to cut and shape it. We must return to Valdah.'

Three hours later Father Sebastian returned again to the graveyard to complete his gory task. He was passed on the road by an ancient coach pulled by two black horses. When he reached the grave, it was again empty. Toomis, the dwarf, had also vanished from the house and it was not difficult to know who had removed the body, together with many of the treasures of the house.

A week later, Martha Hoffman was well enough to travel and she, Eric and I left Valdah to return to our homes.

I still receive the occasional letter from Father Sebastian. Valdah has not again been troubled by vampires, though there is no certainty that the Count might not, one day, return to that unfortunate village.

Meanwhile, he may be anywhere in this world, perhaps known only as a rich, eccentric whose one servant is an ugly dwarf called Toomis.

45

The dwarf's speech became worse.

'You prom – promise me be 'ike you. Many time, you p'omise Toomis.'

'Many times, you have asked,' replied the Count. 'Never had I made such a promise.'

There was now no mistaking the expression on the dwarf's face. It was one of sheer desperation. He picked up the lamp and knelt with it in front of his master.

'You p'omise me!' he shouted, again and again.

The Count struck him across the face. Toomis fell to the ground, the oil lamp breaking beneath him. The flames began to leap up. It was as if Toomis was unaware of what had happened. He grasped the Count about the legs, still shouting the same words. The Count tried to free himself, but now both were in flames.

As the flames leapt higher, there was a cracking in the timbers above. A great beam fell upon the burning figures, its rotten wood splintering around them and bursting into new flame.

I ran up the stairs leading out of the crypt, already choking with the smoke which filled the air. The heavy door would not move. It was locked. I could not find the key which Margheta had given me. More of the roof was crumbling. In a moment, I would be trapped. I must find the other stairs!

I ran across the floor of the crypt, past all that remained of the blazing figures, still locked together as the flames consumed them.

I was met only with another wall of flame and no way through it. I knew that I was trapped.

What little air might be left would be near the floor. I lay on the stones gasping at the last traces of life-giving air. Something clattered onto the stone; the key to the crypt door. I stretched out my hand and clutched it in my fingers, but it was too late. I no longer had the strength even to crawl across the floor.

Perhaps Valdah would be grateful to me for destroying its vampire, but the credit was not mine. This thing of evil had been destroyed by the simple love and devotion of a twisted mind inside a twisted body.